SCARY TALES

I SCREAM,
YOU SCREAM!

JAMES PRELLER
SCARY TALES
I SCREAM, YOU SCREAM!

Illustrated by IACOPO BRUNO

MACMILLAN CHILDREN'S BOOKS

First published in the US 2013 by Feiwel and Friends

This edition published 2013 by Macmillan Children's Books
a division of Macmillan Publishers Limited
20 New Wharf Road, London N1 9RR
Basingstoke and Oxford
Associated companies throughout the world.
www.panmacmillan.com

ISBN 978-1-4472-4687-9

35798642

A CIP catalogue record for this book is available from
the British Library.

Book design by Ashley Halsey
Printed and bound by CPI Group (UK) Ltd, Croydon CR0 4YY

For Jen Steil,
great teacher, friend, book-lover, and inspiration.
Thanks for your support and enthusiasm over the years.

CONTENTS

I SCREAM.

YOU SCREAM

WE ALL
SCREAM!

ENTER THE WORLD OF SAMANTHA CARVER – AN ORDINARY KID WHO LOVES AMUSEMENT PARKS, THE SMELL OF POPCORN, AND THE TERROR OF A HEART-POUNDING RIDE.

SAM'S GOT A TICKET IN HER POCKET FOR A VERY SPECIAL RIDE. SOON THIS TICKET, RIPPED IN HALF, WILL SIGNAL THE BEGINNING OF A MOST UNUSUAL ADVENTURE. IT WILL LEAVE SAM, ALONG WITH A BOY NAMED ANDY, SCREAMING FOR THEIR LIVES.

SO COME ALONG. TAKE A SEAT. BUCKLE UP, NICE AND TIGHT. IT'S SURE TO BE A BUMPY RIDE. AND IF YOU NEED ANYTHING – ANYTHING AT ALL – JUST SCREAM.

DR Z'S
ADVENTURE PARK

The Carvers stood first in line for the grand opening of the Dragon Tooth, advertised as the greatest thrill ride in amusement park history. Samantha gazed back at the zigzag of customers, people of every shape, size, and colour. She couldn't believe her good luck.

The word 'excited' didn't exactly describe Sam's feelings. She was ecstatic, overjoyed, tweaked, gonzo, completely over the moon.

Her hands fluttered like hummingbirds, darting up to her thick black hair, drifting skyward, then diving down into her pockets.

Who could blame her? Sam was visiting her favourite place on the planet: Doctor Z's Adventure Park. No one loved amusement parks more than eleven-year-old Sam Carver. She loved everything about them. The crowds, the food, the noise – music blaring, bells dinging, children screaming,

'I SCREAM, YOU SCREAM, WE ALL SCREAM ON ROLLER COASTERS!'

Sammy loved the buttery smell of popcorn that filled her nostrils, the sweetness of candyfloss, the grease of hot dogs and burgers. But most of all, she loved the rides, every single one – the Whirligig and the Wheel of Wonder, the Windseeker and Skyscreamer, the Gravitron and Ricochet and Cloud

Chaser. She worshipped the Wall of Death and dearly loved the Spiral of Doom.

For Sam, there was only one rule: the scarier, the better. And after each ride, Sam would cry: 'Again, again, again!'

She checked – once again, for the hundredth time – for the thick, cardboard ticket in the front pocket of her dress. She bounced on her heels in anticipation. Her eyes lifted to watch a red-tailed hawk glide through the clouds. *Bird in the sky*, she thought, *I know how you feel*.

'I'm sooooo excited!' Sam told her parents. 'I feel like a bottle of soda, all fizzy inside, ready to pop.'

'Try not to explode,' her father said. 'That might be messy.'

Mrs Carver looked up from her folded newspaper. She enjoyed word games, and completed the crossword puzzle every

morning. Sam liked to help her mother solve the Daily Jumble and play with anagrams, where you rearranged the letters of one word to form new words.

She pretended her own name, Samantha, was an anagram.

A HATS MAN.
ASH MAN AT.
HAM ANT AS.

Oh well, it was a disappointing list.

Sam was certain that today was going to be the best day of her life. She turned to her parents and beamed a smile of pure sunshine. 'Thanks for bringing me, Mom and Dad. I can't believe how happy I am.'

Months before, Sam had entered a contest by clicking on a link and, amazingly, despite the odds, actually won a prize. Her reward?

A ticket to be among the first customers to enjoy the Greatest Thrill Ride Ever Created. But was Sam brave enough?

Oh yes, surely she was. Nothing frightened Sam Carver. Nothing, that is, except for dentists, bats, and homework. The usual things. Dentists, of course, with their fat fingers fumbling in your mouth. But bats creeped Sam out the most, with their leathery wings and tiny teeth and weird human faces.

Besides, homework scared everybody!

THE THIN MAN IN A DULL BLACK SUIT

Behind the entrance gate, a man sat upon a high stool, legs crossed, fingers knotted on his lap. He appeared to Sam like a grim vulture, a strange and hostile bird of prey.

Sam could see that he was unusually tall, with long arms and legs jutting out at awkward angles. A lanky man dressed in a faded black suit, plain white shirt, and narrow tie. His shoes were scuffed and battered.

The man had a sharp nose, a down-turned mouth, and restless eyes that never stopped moving.

The man guarded a door that led into a huge, warehouse-size building. *Ginormous*, Sam thought. On the wall was the painted head of a massive dragon, yellow eyes gleaming with menace, teeth sharp as knives. In exotic letters that almost looked Chinese, a sign read,

THE DRAGON TOOTH

According to articles that Sam had read on the Internet, this particular ride had been in development for more than five years, and was considered the crown jewel of Dr Z's empire. Details were top secret. No one knew whether it would be a new kind of roller coaster or . . . or . . . it could be anything! Part

of the fun for Sam had been imagining what the ride might possibly be.

'Maybe they drop you from, like, a million feet in the air,' Sam speculated.

'Sounds high.' Her father whistled.

'Or maybe it's like one of those slingshot things, like something with bungee cords, or with crazy g-forces, or . . .'

Sam could see that her father was bored. While Mrs Carver patiently filled in the boxes of her crossword puzzle, Sam's father sweated in the summer heat, and squeezed the back of his neck. He checked the time on his mobile and frowned. 'We've been waiting almost two hours,' he groaned. 'Ever since my time in the army, I promised myself I'd never stand in line again.'

Sam shot her father a look. 'It's OK, Dad. The ride will be totally worth it.'

'I don't know, kiddo,' her father replied

wearily. 'I feel pretty silly standing around like this.'

The thin man cleared his throat with a growl. 'Patience,' he murmured.

He glanced at the sky. A flicker of worry flashed in his eyes. A change in light caused Sam's eyes, too, to lift skyward. As if the air had shifted somehow, as if the sky changed colour. It happened fast, in a blink, but it felt impossibly . . . **WRONG**. Even worse, Sam felt as if she was being observed by someone, or something. A camera in the sky, a watchful eye. Sam scolded herself for being a goofball, and decided to think happier thoughts.

Sam looked around. No one else seemed to notice anything, except for the man in the dark suit. His gaze kept returning to the sky, lips pursed thoughtfully. He had the nervous habit of rubbing a thumb against the crook of his forefinger.

'Excuse me, sir? Will you be letting us in soon?' Sam asked.

The man made no reply.

Sam pressed forward. 'Do you know what the ride is like? Have you seen it?'

He now directed his cold gaze at Sam. 'I have,' he said. 'You will not be disappointed.'

'Have you met Dr Z?' she persisted.

The man smiled, but without warmth. 'Ah, the mysterious Dr Z. What do you know about the owner of this amusement park?'

'Lots,' Sam said. 'He's one of the most mysterious men in the world. His real name is Phineas Z. Overstreet. And he's a reclusive, eccentric billionaire!'

'Eccentric,' the man replied. 'A big word for "crazy".'

Sam laughed. 'He's brilliant, and lives in his own world. He won't let anyone take his picture. And he's crazy about games, just like me.' She knew that Mr Overstreet made his fortune as an inventor. Then the sky did it again. As if the clouds had rearranged, or somehow the planet tilted in a new direction. All in the sliver of an instant. But Sam noticed. She glanced at the man in the dark suit. He sensed it too. Sam could see it in his eyes, and in the way his fingers twitched.

She noticed something else, too. An absence. 'There are no birds,' she said, turning to her father. 'I don't see any, Dad. I don't hear them. They're all gone.'

'I guess they flew the coop,' Mr Carver replied.

'There were lots of birds before,' Sam insisted. 'Sparrows by the gardens, and red-winged blackbirds. I was watching them before. I saw a hawk too. But now—'

'I'm sure it's nothing, kiddo,' Mr Carver said.

SAM ENTERS THE DRAGON

A pale-faced boy with limp, white-blond hair appeared beside Sam. He looked sickly. He was a few years younger than Sam and stood strangely erect. In a flat voice, he said, 'I am ready now, sir.'

Sam laughed to herself. What a strange thing to say. Everyone was ready. More than ready.

The thin man nodded, offered a wafer-thin smile. 'Noted,' he intoned, drawing out the vowel sounds. 'However, there have been disturbances, difficulties with the satellites, computer malfunctions.' He pointed a bony finger upward, beyond the clouds, to deep space. 'Please stand by. We apologize for any inconvenience.'

The pale boy stood by as requested.

'It won't be long,' the thin man added. He pressed a forefinger to his ear and closed his eyes as if listening to a message. After a moment, the man unfolded his long limbs, like a great mantis, and stood before the crowd.

With a hand to the side of his mouth, he announced, 'Welcome to the grand opening of the Dragon Tooth, the single greatest ride in the world's greatest amusement park – Dr Z's Adventure Park!'

The crowd burst into applause. A large man in a too-small shirt put two fat sausage-like fingers in his mouth and whistled.

A pained expression appeared on the face of the man in the black suit. He signalled for silence. 'Before we begin, please, a word.' He glanced at the words scribbled on a scrap of paper in his hand, then returned the paper to his jacket pocket.

'Adventure Park was established eleven years ago by Phineas Z. Overstreet.' The man coughed once and continued. 'Mr Overstreet was a sickly child who spent long hours in solitude. To ease his loneliness, he read voraciously and tinkered with computers. He earned his first million by the age of twelve, with the invention of a popular video game. By the time he was seventeen, his company, Z-GAMES, had become the largest, bestselling game company in the world. At thirty-two, Phineas Z. Overstreet was the wealthiest man on the planet.

'And he was bored – bored with work,

bored with meetings, bored with money. So he built his greatest game of all and called it Adventure Park!'

The crowd applauded.

'The rides feature cutting-edge technology, innovative designs, and – ah, yes – the most terrifying thrills. Today, you will witness Dr Z's greatest achievement, a ride that goes beyond anything the world has witnessed.'

His eyes turned to Sam's direction. 'Am I correct to assume that you have a winning ticket?'

Sam placed the ticket in the man's hand. He ripped it in half and let the pieces flutter to the ground. But when Sam's parents also moved forward, he raised an open palm. 'The ticket is for one rider only.'

'Yes, of course,' Mrs Carver said, 'but we figured we could step inside to—'

'Incorrect. False,' the man snapped. 'You are mistaken.'

Mrs Carver put a hand on Sam's shoulder. 'Can't we go inside, just to watch?'

'No, that would be . . . impossible,' the man replied. 'Imprudent. Immaterial. Impractical. The ride is not on the premises, exactly.'

'Not on the . . . what?'

He bent forward at the waist, hands clasped behind his back. He whispered, 'Mr Overstreet would have me sacked in an instant – kicked to the kerb – if I were to allow you inside. You must understand. He is fiercely protective of industry secrets. But I can say this. First, there is a brief shuttle that will transport your daughter to the ride itself, which is at a different location.'

'I don't under—'

'Mom, it's OK,' Sam interrupted. She

appealed to her father. 'Tell her, Dad. I'll be fine, really.'

Her parents exchanged glances. Their daughter alone? Unwatched?

'She will be quite safe,' the man purred. 'You'll need to sign the standard paperwork, waivers and such, for insurance purposes. Of course, if you wish to forfeit the ticket, I'm sure others will happily take her place.'

So it was decided. The man unhooked a chain, opened a door, and Sam stepped inside. The line inched forward. A total of sixteen riders entered the building. The boy was among them, his skin as white as a sheet.

All the riders were children.

Sam didn't look back at her parents. Didn't wave goodbye. Instead, full of anticipation, she walked into the cavernous room – excited, hopeful, not the least bit fearful of the dangers that would soon fall from the sky.

THINGS GO VERY WRONG

Sam was harnessed into an open, two-seated vehicle. It looked like an old coal-mining car, big wheels on a primitive track. Nothing fancy about it. Sam felt a pang of disappointment. This wasn't what she'd expected.

Next to her sat the pale-faced boy. Up close, Sam noticed that his skin was flawless, perfectly smooth. He never looked Sam in the eyes. There was something else too, something stiff about his manner. He stared forward as if he was waiting for a bus.

Two workers in orange flight suits walked around, checking on the eight cars, making sure each passenger was safely strapped in.

Sam glanced around the warehouse. It was grey, almost plain. 'Is this . . . it?' she asked a bearded worker.

He laughed. 'No worries, missy. We haven't put in all the finishing touches. Grand openings are like that. This here is only a shuttle car that will carry you through a tunnel of solid rock. When you arrive at the loading zone, my colleagues will lead you into a high tower. No one can see this tower from the road, by the way, because it looks exactly like a massive oak tree.' He flashed a gold tooth. 'That's when you enter the dragon's mouth.'

He jabbed a wicker basket in Sam's direction. 'No mobiles.'

'Really?'

'Really,' the man confirmed. 'Messes with the electronics, like on aeroplanes. Besides, Mr Overstreet does not allow photography.'

Sam reluctantly placed her phone in the basket. The mobile represented Sam's connection to her parents and friends. By handing over the phone, Sam said goodbye to the outside world.

'Ready?' the man asked.

Before Sam could answer, the car lurched forward and her back pressed against the seat.

They clanked and rattled along the track. The car sloped down into an underground tunnel, lit by green floor lights.

Sam liked the fluorescent lights and the trapped feeling of the tunnel; she felt like she was being swallowed by a great beast. 'This is cool.' She smiled at the boy.

He didn't answer, just gripped the front rail of the car.

'I'm Sammy or Sam, just not Samantha. Oh, I don't care. Take your pick!' she said cheerfully. 'What's your name?'

Sam saw his lips move. But she couldn't hear a word the boy said. The explosions were too deafening.

Sam's ears rang from the noise. Startled, she tried to turn in her seat, locate the source of the blasts, but the harness was too tight. The boy tilted his head forward, hands over his ears, eyes closed. Clouds of smoke and grit began to fill the tunnel. He coughed softly.

Could this be the ride? Sam wondered. It didn't seem right. She pulled the top of her shirt over her mouth to keep out the smoke. Sam recalled the sky, how it had shimmered strangely just before they entered the warehouse. Her feeling of being watched from above. Then came another explosion, louder than before. A jagged crack formed on

the ceiling. Large chunks of rock and granite crashed behind them.

Sam yanked fiercely at her harness, pulling an arm through and twisting herself around. She saw that they were cut off from the rest of the passenger cars. Separated by an avalanche of rock. She heard screams, muffled from behind the fallen rocks. They were the screams of frightened and desperate children, who might be injured, bleeding, buried alive.

'Something has gone wrong. This should not be happening,' the boy said. He clutched at Sam's hand. His fear charged through Sam's body like an electric current. 'Those kids back there . . .'

He dared not finish the sentence.

Sam knew he was right.

Something had gone terribly wrong.

And the car rolled on through the smoke-filled dark.

'RUN, JUST RUN!'

It took only two more minutes, but to Sam the trip lasted forever. Finally the car reached the loading zone, where they were supposed to begin the ride for real. Go up the tower, have fun.

Not today.

A woman in an orange jumpsuit had her back to them. She aimed a fire extinguisher at a wall of flames. A man, also in orange, lay on the ground. He was partly covered in fallen rocks. One leg was bent out at an unnatural angle. A puddle of blood oozed beneath his head.

Sam wriggled to escape from the harness. Finally she twisted free. She turned to the boy. 'Try to get out. We can't stay here.'

He sat paralysed, perfectly still. Another explosion hit from above. The ground shook. Sam thought she heard the distant **WHIRRR** of a dentist's drill. A high-pitched whine. She pulled frantically at the boy's harness. Nothing worked. 'I'll get help.'

'No, do not leave me!' he pleaded. But Sam raced off towards the woman with the fire extinguisher.

At Sam's approach, the woman turned and stared with a look of disbelief. Blood pulsed from an open gash on her forehead. Her eyes lingered briefly on the bloodied man on the floor. The woman shouted above the din, 'I didn't think anyone made it through!'

Sam pointed to the boy in the car. 'I can't get him out!'

The woman turned back to the fire, and with a sweeping motion laid down a spray of white foam. Another explosion rocked the walls. A crack in the shape of a lightning bolt crawled across the ceiling. The woman cast a wary look at it, calculating their odds of survival.

'You have to get out now!' the woman told Sam.

'What's happened?' Sam yelled. 'I don't understand.'

The woman shook her head. 'I can't explain. Some kind of attack. Reports say that it's happening all over the city, like the sky is falling. Asteroids, meteors, bombs, I don't know.' She pushed Sam by the shoulder. 'Go, run. That hallway will take you to the woods.'

Sam paused. 'What about you?'

The woman shook her head. Hoisted the fire extinguisher. 'You first,' she shouted. Again, she pushed Sam away. 'I'll get out soon.'

Sam's feet carried her towards the exit. Then she stopped, glanced back at the boy still trapped in the car. He looked so helpless.

'Do you have a knife?' Sam shouted at the woman.

She stared back blankly, blood trickling down her cheek. The woman didn't understand.

Sam made a desperate, back-and-forth motion with her hand. 'Something to cut with!'

The woman blinked and pointed to a table against the wall. Sam raced to the desk, whipped open one drawer after another. *There!* She grabbed a box cutter and ran back to the boy.

The cutter was sharp and worked well.

Still, the boy seemed too frightened to move. The room grew hotter, flames warming the rock walls like a furnace. Sam grabbed the boy's shoulders and shook him. 'Come on,' she urged. 'I know the way out.'

The boy shook his head. *No, no, no.*

There was no time for this. Sam slapped the boy across the cheek. The boy's eyes rolled in his head, then settled on Sam's face, as if he was snapping awake from a dream. Or a nightmare. 'Trust me,' Sam said in the calmest voice she could muster. 'I promise to protect you. But we have to go *now*.'

And so they moved past the woman and beyond the chaos of the loading zone. They fled down a hallway, out a heavy metal exit door, and into the woods.

Once outside in the open air, Sam fell to her knees, coughing, tears filling her eyes from the stress and smoke. After a moment, she felt the boy's hand on her shoulders. He prodded at her. 'Look up,' he said, pointing.

Through the stand of tall trees, beyond the leafy branches, Sam saw a massive shape in the sky, large enough to blot out the sun. Lights, like lasers, spiked out from it in all directions, like spokes from a wheel. It took Sam a full minute to comprehend what she was seeing, and yet she still could not believe it. Finally, the words formed in her mind.

I am looking at a spaceship, Sam thought.

And then Samantha Carver remembered her parents.

She reached for her mobile. But her pocket was empty. She had given it to the man back there, dropped it into a basket a world away.

Sam recalled the terrified boy beside her, and her promise to protect him.

Sam's last thought, before she rose to her feet, was only this:

RUN.
RUN, OR DIE.

So she grabbed the boy's hand, tugged.

And together they ran.

SAFE, FOR NOW

They were in a forest of tall, mature trees. Pine needles and roots covered the ground. Here and there, branches crashed and fell. Sam stopped beside a thick tree and looked up. Lasers from the spaceship strafed the ground in a steady, rhythmic pattern. Back and forth, back and forth. Massive trees splintered like toothpicks. Small fires sprinkled across the forest floor.

Sam felt her legs grow weak. It was difficult

to breathe. She could not escape the sense that a great eye watched them from above. As if she was starring in someone's disaster movie.

From the corner of one eye, Sam spied an alien creature loping in the distance, moving swiftly through the trees on multiple legs. It was unlike any creature Sam had ever seen. Not man, not beast – but **THING.**

Sam's heart pounded so hard, she feared it might burst in her chest.

How could this be happening?

There was no time to think.

No time to figure it out.

'This way!' the boy whispered urgently. He seemed alert now, recovered from the shock. The boy ran about ten feet in the opposite direction of the creature, stopped, and waved for Sam to follow.

Sam heard a crack, looked up, and dived out of the way, rolling and tumbling on the

ground. A massive branch fell where she'd been standing.

The boy pulled her up.

He raced to a thicket of undergrowth, dived to the ground, and tunnelled through on his belly with her close behind. Branches snagged and scratched at Sam's skin. They reached the side of a rocky cliff that rose skyward. There was nowhere to turn. The boy seemed uncertain. Sam stepped forward and said, 'This way.' She forged a path to the right. After twenty feet, Sam found a crevice in a rock wall. It was big enough for them to squeeze inside.

'Are you sure?' the boy asked.

'Nope,' Sam answered, and she led the way inside.

They stood together in the dim half-light, their chests heaving. They were inside a cave.

Sam inched away from the mouth of the cave, putting distance between herself and . . .

that thing outside, roaming the woods.

IT.
WHATEVER IT WAS.

The boy whimpered softly. He sagged against the cave wall, arms hugging his knees. Rocking back and forth.

Sam hushed the boy. 'Quiet.'

The boy flinched, as if he'd been slapped.

'Shhh, easy,' Sam said again, softer this time, kinder. 'I think we'll be safe here.'

He shook his head. His eyes looked too round and wide, almost inhuman, like the eyes of a captured bird in a cat's mouth.

'What's your name?' she asked, hoping to calm the boy. 'You never told me.'

The boy looked at her as if he didn't understand the question. His head tilted to the side, as if puzzling out a maths equation.

'I'm Sam,' she reminded him.

'Dinardo,' the boy said. 'My name is Andy Dinardo the Third.'

Sam almost laughed. *The Third*. Mr Fancy Pants. Probably a rich kid, not like Sam. A lot of good that would do him now, cowering in a cave, trying not to get killed.

'Andy Dinardo the Third,' Sam echoed. 'It's nice to meet you.'

Andy shifted on his backside, stretched out his legs. He grimaced, and Sam noticed that the sleeve of his left arm was torn. 'Are you hurt? Let me see.'

'No,' the boy said, clasping a hand over the ripped sleeve. He pulled away from her. 'Just scratches,' Andy insisted. 'I do not like to be touched.'

'Sure,' Sam said. 'Whatever. Just don't get all weird on me. We've got enough problems.'

ANOTHER WAY OUT

The high-pitched drone continued outside the cave. Then came a series of crunching sounds, and the crashing of trees.

Something horrible was happening. Something

UNEARTHLY.

'What is that out there?' the boy wondered.

Sam shook her head. She remembered the words of the woman in the loading zone.

'*Some kind of attack*,' the woman had said. '*It's . . . like the sky is falling. Asteroids, meteors, bombs . . .*'

Sam wondered if the woman made it out alive. They didn't wait around to find out.

Could it be an invasion? Aliens?

That was crazy, impossible.

But . . . that thing in the sky.

The faces of Sam's parents flashed in her mind. Were they OK? Were they searching for her even now? Sam missed her mobile. It was like a lifeline that connected Sam to the outside world, and now Sam felt cut off, adrift . . . like floating in a wild sea . . . lost, frightened, and alone.

The boy coughed, moaned softly. Sam reminded herself that she had made a promise. **I MUST BE BRAVE**, she thought. For the boy. He was so different from her. Andy was pale and weak; Sam was dark-skinned and athletic. He was quiet and fearful; Sam felt confident, able. He was young and he needed her help. Sam was strong, and she would be able to give it.

'You OK, Andy?' Sam asked.

The boy nodded, rubbing the front of his neck. 'A little thirsty, I guess.'

Water. Sam hadn't thought about it, but the moment he mentioned his thirst, she became aware of the dryness of her own throat. She suddenly felt exhausted, wanting to close her eyes and wake up in her comfortable bed to a new day.

The boy said something.

'What?'

'Thank you,' Andy repeated.

Sam turned to him, surprised.

'For before,' he said. 'Back at the ride. You could have left me.'

'And miss your awesome company?' Sam joked. 'Anybody would have done the same thing.'

Andy wasn't so sure, but he smiled in that odd, crooked way of his.

'I wish we had a torch or a lighter,' Sam said, thinking out loud. 'We could explore this cave. Maybe find a safer way out.'

'I have a little flashlight on my key chain,' the boy offered.

'You do? Really? That's *awesome*! I mean, that's like *exactly* what we need right now.'

Andy dropped the flashlight in Sam's hand. It was a smooth metallic cylinder about the size of a small pen, but its beam was surprisingly powerful.

Sam directed the beam into the darkness, deeper into the gloom. It illuminated parts of the cave which appeared to be vast enough for Andy and Sam to stand upright in. 'What do you think? Want to look around?' Sam asked.

Andy paused, uncertain.

They needed to get moving. Now.

Sam realized that Andy was too young to make those decisions. He could sit and wait for hours. But they needed water. The loud, mysterious noises continued outside the cave.

'Take my hand,' Sam said.

She led the way deeper into the cave, deeper into the dark unknown.

THE CEILING IS ALIVE!

The two children, strangers just a few hours ago, slowly picked their way through the tunnel of the cave. At times it grew narrow, with the moist cave walls brushing against Sam's shoulders. They waded through puddles, splashing in a stream of ankle-deep water. Sam's teeth chattered against the cold. She shivered, paused, and looked back at Andy.

'You all right?'

He nodded.

Sam smiled. *He's a good kid*, she thought. *Very quiet. Doesn't complain. Tries hard to be brave.*

'Tell me about you,' Sam said.

'About me?' Andy echoed.

'Yeah. I mean, I didn't see you with anybody. Who brought you to the park?'

'My . . . father,' Andy said after a moment. 'He does not like rides.'

Sam laughed. 'Ha! My dad's the same way. He says that he'd rather clean a toilet bowl with a toothbrush than go on another roller coaster.'

The tight passageway opened up to a large cavern with a ceiling at least fifteen feet high.

'Wow,' Sam said. 'Look at this place.'

Andy looked, as requested.

'But what's that disgusting smell?' Sam complained.

She moved the beam to the rock floor. It was covered in some kind of thick, greenish slime. It smelt rank. Sam worked hard not to gag.

A steady trickle of droplets hit the rock floor, **PLINK, PLINK, PLINK.** 'Do you hear that?' Sam asked. 'Could it be water falling from a stalactite?'

'No, not water,' Andy said. 'I think it is called *guano*.'

'Guano?'

'Bat droppings.'

Sam gulped. *Bats*. She hated bats.

Sam aimed the flashlight at the ceiling and stepped back in horror. The ceiling was alive. The roof of the cave was writhing, squirming, crawling with hundreds – no, thousands upon thousands – of bats. The bodies of mice, with human faces. Sam felt woozy, on the edge of panic.

This was worse than homework.

Way worse.

9

ANDY'S PLAN

'I know about bats,' Andy said.

Sam tried to swallow. There was no saliva in her mouth. Her eyes stayed fixed on the ceiling, where thousands of bats slept upside down, crawled, or shivered inside their wings. Guano dripped, dripped, dripped from the ceiling.

'What if they wake up?' Sam asked.

'Bats are amazing. They use echolocation to navigate in dark places,' the boy said.

'This cave must be their daytime roost. They probably go out at dusk, thousands of them at a time, like a ribbon of black smoke in the sky.'

Andy shouted suddenly, 'Bats, awake!'

His voice bounced off the walls and echoed back, back, back.

The bats stirred. A groggy few left their upside-down perch.

'Are you crazy?' Sam whispered.

'We need to wake them,' Andy insisted. 'The bats know how to get out of here. They will lead us to the light.'

'No, no, no-no-no, no.' Sam waved her hands in protest. 'We can't, I won't. I can't have those disgusting things flying around, getting in my hair . . .'

Her skin crawled at the thought.

But even as she argued, Sam realized that Andy was right. The bats might help. Sam took a deep breath. 'OK, I get it. But I want you to know that this idea totally, totally freaks me out.'

Andy directed Sam to check the floor with the flashlight. He found two slime-covered rocks and handed one to Sam. 'On three,' he said, 'we throw the rocks and scream as loud as we can.'

'Great, we're bat alarm clocks,' Sam muttered.

'**ONE** . . .'

'I sooooo hate this,' Sam complained.

'**TWO** . . .'

'I'd rather do maths homework . . . for a week,' Sam said.

'**THREE!**'

Sam threw the rock, and screamed her head off.

'**AAAAAHHHHH!**'

She covered her head with both hands, scrunched down, and squeezed her eyes shut.

But Sammy could not stop the terrifying noises from filling her ears. Instantly, the cave came alive with the scratching sounds of claws scrambling on rock, like mice scurrying across stone floors . . . the thrum of leathery wings . . . and the high-pitched, deafening screech of a thousand bats in chaotic flight.

'Quick!' Andy yanked at Sam's shoulder. 'We must follow them!'

10

FALLING, FALLING

It was amazing. Even beautiful, in a way. The bats flapped and flew to the far end of the cavern and spiralled up and up, through a shaft of light.

Andy raced ahead. 'A ladder!'

Sammy reached Andy's side. They high-fived in triumph. 'You're a genius, Andy Dinardo the Third,' Sam said. 'Way to go!'

The boy actually smiled.

It was an ancient ladder, slats of wood hammered into the rock ages ago.

'Who built this?' Sam wondered. 'Miners?'

'Do you think it's safe?' Andy asked.

Sam reached for the outside edge of a board. She pulled hard. *Crack*. The dry, brittle wood snapped off in her hand.

'I will go first,' Andy said.

'No,' Sam protested. 'I don't want you to get hurt.'

'I am lighter,' Andy argued.

'But I am bigger than you,' Sammy countered. 'I'm going first. Unless you want to fight about it?'

Andy said nothing.

'Don't worry,' Sam said. 'I'll take it slow.'

Sam looked up the shaft. It climbed at least twenty-five feet to the earth floor above. She could feel a downward draft of air, a slight breeze on her face. *Air, light*. There was only one safe way out – and that was up.

She took a first step, then another. The

ladder held. Up and up, she climbed, slow and steady.

'You are doing great,' Andy called.

He seemed far away. She glanced down, which was not a good idea. She felt light-headed, as images turned and tumbled in her mind. Sam's foot slipped . . .

But Sammy held on, muscles burning. She shook the cobwebs from her brain, and found another foothold. She took a step up. And another. One by one, step by step. Up and up.

When she reached the top, Sam sprawled with her back on the ground, arms and legs out like a snow angel. The sky was quiet. There were no more explosions. Fresh air filled her lungs.

'Sam? Sammy?' the boy called.

'All clear!' Sam yelled down. 'Come on up. You can do it. Nice and slow.'

While she waited and hoped, Sam

distracted herself by playing with anagrams. She tried the word 'Andy.' The trick was to use all the letters in one new word, or at least in a clever sentence.

ANY, DAY, NAY . . .

Samantha frowned. She couldn't find a way to use all four letters. Maybe 'Dinardo' would work better.

ADD IRON.
ODD RAIN.
DAD IN OR . . .

Andy's hand reached the top rung. Sam pulled him up by the elbow. He made it!

They made it.

Together.

After a moment, Andy asked, 'Which way now?'

Sam shook her head. 'No idea.'

A noise came from the distance, the crashing of a tree.

They decided to walk the other way. And quickly.

After a short walk, Sam spied a steep ravine and a small stream below. 'Water,' she said.

Andy didn't hesitate. He scrambled down the ravine, grabbing tree roots for balance, sending dirt and stones tumbling downhill as he went.

'Slow down,' Sam warned. She took a few cautious steps and reached out to grab on to a large rock for balance. 'You could easily fall and—'

The unstable rock shuddered and rolled away beneath Sam's hand.

It happened in an instant.

Enough time for Sam to think, *Uh-oh*.

And next she was rag-dolling down the

ravine, plummeting head over heels past Andy, rolling towards a stand of trees.

With amazing speed, Andy lunged in front of Sam. He wrapped his arms around her torso and they rolled like a ball into the tree. Andy braced his right arm and took the full force of the impact against the tree trunk.

The sound was terrible.

Andy's arm below the elbow shattered like glass.

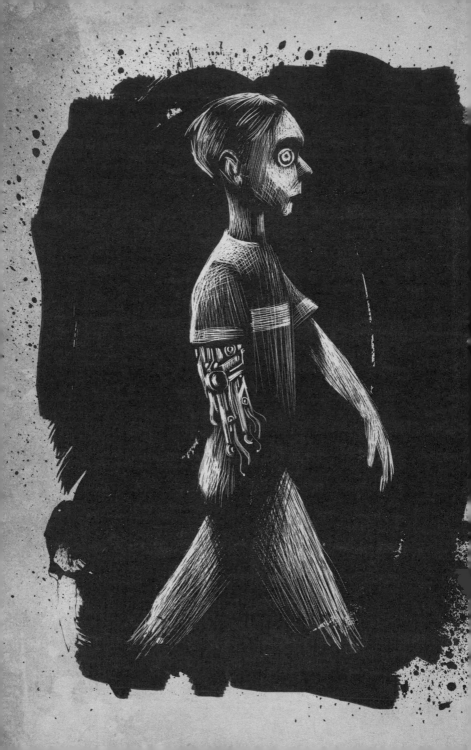

WIRES

Sam tried to clear her dizzy, throbbing head. Her banged and bruised body ached. She opened and closed her fingers, tested her legs, opened her eyes. Nothing was broken.

Andy sat perfectly calm, leaning against the tree trunk.

He cradled the injured arm in his free hand. The only hand he had left.

His other hand was shattered in the fall.

But instead of flesh and bones and blood, Sam saw metal rods, wires, and tiny lights.

The insides of his arm looked like a computer.

Stunned, Sam crab-walked away in horror, stumbling backwards, scrambling up the slope.

'Wait, Sam!' Andy cried. He stepped closer.

'Stay away from me!' Sam screamed.

Andy dropped back, sitting down quietly.

Sam couldn't speak. She stared at Andy's arm. She saw, too, that his face was bruised in the fall, and a flap of skin by his eye was torn off. Beneath it, she saw wires and more metal.

The letters of the anagram jumbled in Sam's mind. In a flash, **DINARDO** turned into **ANDROID**.

'You're not . . . you're not human,' Sammy stammered.

'I am sorry. It was not supposed to be this way,' Andy said. 'I have failed.'

'What are you?' Sam asked.

'A friend,' Andy said.

Sam shook her head, no. She stood, stepped away, and prepared to run.

Suddenly a loud pop, like a fireworks display, exploded high in the sky. But instead of colourful lights, dazzling letters appeared against the clouds.

The letters formed words.

The words read: GAME OVER.

12

OVERSTREET

Samantha Carver and Andy Dinardo the Third—the robot boy, or android, or whatever he was — walked together in the peaceful forest.

Andy knew the way, and Sam followed.

The game was over.

Sam had not realized it had been a game all along.

Andy said, 'My assignment was to keep you safe.'

'*You* were protecting *me*?' Sam said. 'I thought *I* was the one who saved *you*. Remember?'

Andy glanced at Sam. He looked down, almost in shame. 'That is what I wanted you to believe.'

They walked for twenty minutes, most of it in silence. 'Where are you taking me?' Sam demanded.

Andy stopped. 'We have arrived.' He pointed to a cabin in the woods. It was a small, ramshackle place, with only one window and a door. A whisper of smoke curled from the chimney. 'All your questions will soon be answered.'

He turned to look at Sam, with his human-like face made of synthetic plastic, wires, chips, and flashing lights. 'I am sorry,' he said. He gestured with his arm. 'You were not meant to see me this way.'

Sam couldn't help but marvel. She was talking to an android. No wonder he had such a peculiar way of speaking. Every word was flattened out, without expression. Now Sam understood why.

'You don't use contractions,' Sam said. '*I am sorry. You were not meant.* I knew there was something weird about the way you talked.'

'It is a bug in the software,' Andy admitted. 'I can not speak in contractions.'

'No, you can't,' Sam said defiantly.

'No, I can not,' he replied, and smiled.

The cabin door squeaked open. It was an invitation. **COME INSIDE.**

Sam looked at Andy. She wasn't sure.

'You once asked me to trust you,' he said. 'Now I ask the same of you. Trust me. I will protect you, always.'

Inside the cabin, the thin man in the black suit sat at a long, wooden table. He was

the man who took Sam's ticket outside the Dragon Tooth.

'Please.' He gestured to an empty chair. 'Sit, Samantha Carver. I have food, lemonade. A phone to call your parents.'

Sam looked at the tray of fruit, sandwiches, and snacks. Her stomach twisted with hunger. She did not sit.

'Who are you?' Sam asked.

'I thought you might have guessed by now,' the man said. 'My name is Phineas Z. Overstreet.'

'The billionaire?'

The man bowed his head. 'At your service. I see you have met my son.'

Sam blinked. She looked to Andy. 'Your son?'

Overstreet grinned, revealing yellow teeth behind thin lips. 'Well, not technically, of course. Andy is an android, as you can see.

His last name, Dinardo, that was a clue we left for you.'

'An anagram,' Sam replied. She sat down at the table. Reached for an Oreo and twisted it open. 'Dinardo, android. I figured it out when I saw his face was made of wires and stuff.'

The man spoke to Andy. 'I see you've sustained an injury, Andrew. You will be repaired at the lab.'

'Are you an android too?' Sam asked.

The man coughed in an odd sort of laughter. 'No,' he answered. 'I am merely a lonely billionaire, shut off from the rest of the world.'

'So you built an android?'

The man nodded. His searching eyes fell on the window, as if fearful of the great world outside, recalling loneliness and cruelty. And at that moment, he seemed impossibly sad. His gaze returned to Sam's face. 'Yes, I created Andy. I think of him as a son.'

'So all this,' Sam said, 'everything that happened to me. The explosions, the avalanche in the tunnel, the spaceship, the bats, the danger. None of it was real?'

'The bats were real,' Overstreet replied. 'Imported from Argentina.'

'What about the dead man covered in blood?' Sam asked. 'The woman with the fire extinguisher?'

'Actors, the blood was red gloop, ketchup or something of the sort,' Overstreet answered.

'And the other kids on the ride? What happened to them?' Sam asked.

Overstreet tilted his head sideways. His eyes flickered with mischief. 'They are safe. I suppose you could say they had adventures of their own.'

'The spaceship?'

'A hologram.'

'Where are my parents?' Sam asked.

'They are waiting at a luxury hotel. My treat, of course. Probably sitting by the pool, sipping cool drinks, dangling their toes in the water. It's all been explained to them,' said Phineas Z. Overstreet. 'You can see them as soon as you wish.'

'I wish,' Sam said.

She stood, sighed, and shook her head with weariness. 'I was scared out of my mind. I thought I was going to die. I can't believe that none of it was real.'

'Your bravery was real,' Overstreet said.

'*I am real.*' Andy had been standing against the wall in silence. Now he stepped forward and looked at Sam.

Sam considered the creature that stood before her. An android named Andy Dinardo the Third. He was like Pinocchio, not a real boy, not really. He was a science project made of rods, plastic, chips, and software.

He had no heart.

Sam walked up, looked him in the eye, and hugged the android close to her chest. 'Thank you for protecting me,' she said.

She turned to the lonely man in the dull black suit. 'Mr Overstreet,' she said. 'After I see my parents, I want one more thing.'

'Yes?'

'I want to do it again.'

'Again?' He raised an eyebrow.

She grinned, white teeth gleaming. 'You've created the greatest thrill ride in amusement park history. And I want to go again,' she declared. 'Again, again, again!'

A buzz came from inside Overstreet's jacket pocket. He pulled out a sleek metallic device. 'Yes? I see,' he spoke into it. 'Please send along the helicopter. And what is the status of the new prototype?'

He listened, eyes fixed on Samantha.

'Send an image, please.'

Overstreet jabbed a finger expertly at the device in his hand.

A photograph appeared for his eyes only. His thin lips curled into a smile. 'Very nice. We'll need five hundred more by the first of the month.'

WHERE DOES THE RIDE BEGIN . . .
AND WHEN DOES IT END?

WHAT IS REAL . . . AND WHAT
IS PART OF SOME PLAN WE CAN'T
BEGIN TO COMPREHEND?

DO ANY OF US REALLY KNOW?

AND MIGHT THERE BE, IN SOME
SECRET LABORATORY, A SMALL
ARMY OF ANDROIDS LINED UP IN
TIDY ROWS?

EACH ONE WEARING YOUR FACE?

LOOKING FOR MORE
THRILLS AND CHILLS?

DON'T MISS THE THIRD
SCARY TALES
BOOK . . .

JAMES PRELLER

SCARY TALES

GOOD NIGHT, ZOMBIE

Illustrated by IACOPO BRUNO

IN THE GATHERING DARK OF AUTUMN
TWILIGHT, THREE STUDENTS ENTER
A NEAR-EMPTY ELEMENTARY SCHOOL.
THEY HUSTLE TO FETCH FORGOTTEN
THINGS: BOOKS, ASSIGNMENTS,
BASKETBALL TRAINERS.

THEY ARE NOT FRIENDS. THEY
SCARCELY KNOW EACH OTHER.

BUT THEY WILL SOON BE
TRAPPED INSIDE - DOORS CHAINED,
LOCKED SHUT. IN THE BASEMENT, A
MYSTERIOUS NIGHT JANITOR WAITS.
AND OUTSIDE, MOVING IN THE MIST,
DARK SHAPES SHUFFLE CLOSER, EVER
CLOSER . . .

WALKERS IN THE MIST

Arnold stood by a window at the far end of the library, from which vantage point he could observe the grounds behind the school. Through the mist, he could see the baseball diamond and basketball courts, the swing set and monkey bars, and the jungle gym that looked like an old pirate ship.

The wind was still. Not a leaf stirred. High above, a full moon appeared like a cloudy eye that stared, unblinking, through the mist.

'I wanted to check outside,' Arnold told them. 'After what the night janitor said about, you know, it being dangerous.'

'Yeah, so?' Carter asked.

'Take a look,' Arnold said.

Esme gazed out the window. 'It's hard to see anything.'

'There!' Carter put a hand on Esme's back, and pointed with his free hand.

As Esme's eyes adjusted to the darkness, she began to make out shapes moving through the grounds. Men and women dressed in clothing from olden times and others in tattered rags, all drifting aimlessly through the school playground.

A murder of crows flapped and bickered near the figures, landing on heads and shoulders. None of the dark shapes seemed to mind.

'Their clothes seem so old-fashioned,'

Esme said. 'Like they're dressed up for a fancy party or a dance or—'

'A funeral,' Carter said.

Arnold hesitated, uncertain. 'Those people don't seem normal.' His breath smelt like spearmint gum. He cracked the gum loudly and chewed.

'Nooooope,' Carter agreed.

Could this be real?

Esme saw, or *thought* she saw, through the fog, a crow peck at the face of one of the figures. Again and again, the black scavenger plucked at the man's eyes.

Yet he shuffled along as if he was just a sad, pathetic scarecrow in a cornfield. Couldn't even scare away a crow.

'How come they're out there,' Carter wondered, 'just wandering around in the dark? It's freaky.'

No one dared to guess. But it didn't

look right, they all felt it.

Dozens of figures ambled across the grounds. Listlessly, aimlessly, like school-children at break-time without the energy to play. Some wore puffy dresses, others were dressed in suits and ties. They walked with their arms at their sides, heads pitched forward, as if led by their noses.

'They don't seem *awake*,' Carter said. 'Like they are sleepwalking or—'

'Zombies,' Arnold said.

SCARY TALES

JAMES PRELLER
is an extremely experienced
author of mystery-horror
stories for children. He lives
in New York with his wife,
three kids, two cats and a
golden labradoodle
called Daisy.

IACOPO BRUNO

is a graphic artist and
illustrator who lives in Italy.

OUR BOOKS ARE FRIENDS FOR LIFE.

THIS FISH JUST GOT NASTY!

When Tom's big brother dunks Frankie the goldfish into toxic green gunge, Tom zaps the fish with a battery to bring him back to life! But there's something weird about the new Frankie – he's now a BIG FAT ZOMBIE GOLDFISH with hypnotic powers . . . and he's out for revenge.

TWO BIG FAT FISHY STORIES THAT WILL KEEP YOU HOOKED AND MAKE YOU LAUGH OUT LOUD!

MO O'HARA